KT-409-894

# A Big Surprise for
# Little Card

Charise Mericle Harper

illustrated by

Anna Raff

WALKER BOOKS
AND SUBSIDIARIES
LONDON · BOSTON · SYDNEY · AUCKLAND

Little Card lived in a building with all of his card friends.
Each card had a special job.

TINY

ROUND CARD

GIANT CARD

WIDE CARD

LONG CARD

LITTLE CARD

Wide Card was a postcard.
He couldn't wait to travel.

Round Card was a price tag –
for something important,
she was sure.

Tiny Card was a prize ticket
for a new shiny toy.

Giant Card was a folder for important office work.

Only two cards didn't know what their grown-up jobs would be. Little Card and Long Card were still waiting for their special letters to arrive.

Getting new post was exciting. Maybe *too* exciting.

OOPS!

UMPH!

EEEEH!

SPLAT.

There were letters everywhere.

"Look!" shouted Little Card. "It's my special letter." He read it aloud:
" 'Dear L. C., Congratulations! You are a birthday card. Your training
   starts tomorrow.' "

Yay!

Little Card loved birthday card school.
He was an excellent student.

Wait...

Wait...

Little Card loved everything about birthdays. He loved the decorating, the games,

the cake

and the presents.

Birth - days are a spe-cial day, you're one year old - er, hip hoo - ray!

But most of all Little Card loved the singing. He always sang the loudest.

One day when Little Card came home from school, Long Card was waiting for him.

"Our letters got mixed up," said Long Card. "Look. You're not a birthday card. I am the birthday card."

"Does this mean I have to go to a different school?" asked Little Card. "There's no time for that," said Long Card. "Today is delivery day. It's time to go."

"You'll have fun," said Long Card. "Your job is interesting and exciting." Then she leaned in and whispered, "Just remember, always use a quiet voice."

All aboard!

On the ride over to his new job, Little Card thought
about Long Card's words. Fun? Interesting? Exciting?
That sounded a lot like a birthday.
Suddenly he knew just what to do.

Little Card raced up the path, opened the big front door, and shouted ...

"Shhh," said a man from behind a thick red book. "This is a library."

Oops. Then ...

# HAPPY LIBRARY!

Suddenly a tall lady with fancy boots appeared. It was Miss Penny, the librarian. She sighed and shook her head.

"Come with me," she said.

Little Card followed Miss Penny to her desk.
"This is Alex," said Miss Penny. "And you are her new library card."

"Hi," whispered Alex.

Alex and Little Card liked each other instantly.

# "Happy Library Day!
# Happy Library Day!
# Happy Library Day!"

cheered Little Card.

The library was filled with things to do. There were games to play.

Ta-da!

There were snacks to eat.

"Cookies always taste better after a story," said Alex.

And there was lots of room for decorating.

"It's a rainbow of books," said Alex.

"Let's read them all," said Little Card.

Little Card and Alex read every book in the rainbow,
even the big black book about space.

The library wasn't exactly like a birthday, but it was close.

"Do you know what's missing?" asked Little Card. "A song."

Alex shook her head. "The library is a place for whispering, not for singing," she said.

But Little Card had a song in his heart and he just had to sing it. He took a deep breath, and sang in his quietest whisper:

Miss Penny smiled and gave Little Card a gold star.

When it was time to go, Little Card followed Alex to the checkout desk. While Miss Penny stamped the books, Little Card recited the book promise Alex had taught him.

"We promise to read, respect and return these books," he said.

"And enjoy them, too," added Miss Penny.

"That was as much fun as a birthday," said Little Card.
"It's too bad Happy Library Day is only once a year."

LIBRARY HOURS
MONDAY – SATURDAY
10 AM – 6 PM
HAPPY READING!

"But it's not," said Alex. "LOOK! Happy Library Day is six days a week! Every week! We can come back tomorrow."

"Yay!" shouted Little Card. "That's the best surprise ever."

"And guess what?" whispered Alex. "Tomorrow is Miss Penny's birthday."

Little Card couldn't believe it. Happy Library Day *and* Happy Birthday together, on the same day? That was perfect for a library card who knew all about birthdays.

"Let's have a party," said Little Card.

"I know just who to invite."

If my public library card could talk, he would say,
"Thank you, Vancouver Public Library. You taught me to love books!"

C.M.H.


For Janet.

A.S.R.

First published 2016 by Walker Books Ltd
87 Vauxhall Walk, London SE11 5HJ

2 4 6 8 10 9 7 5 3 1

Text © 2016 Charise Mericle Harper
Illustrations © 2016 Anna Raff
Songs: words and music © 2016 by Anna Raff

The right of Charise Mericle Harper and Anna Raff to be identified as author and illustrator respectively of this work
has been asserted by them in accordance with the Copyright, Designs and Patents Act 1988

This book has been typeset in Billy light

Printed in China

FSC
www.fsc.org

MIX
Paper from
responsible sources
FSC® C012700

British Library Cataloguing in Publication Data:
a catalogue record for this book is available from the British Library

ISBN 978-1-4063-6726-3
www.walker.co.uk